DUCK
LIGHT

GILLIAN A. CORSIATTO
ILLUSTRATED BY ALISON FORSBERG

FriesenPress

Suite 300 - 990 Fort St
Victoria, BC, V8V 3K2
Canada

www.friesenpress.com

Copyright © 2021 by Gillian A. Corsiatto
First Edition — 2021

Additional Contributors:
Jock Mackenzie, Editor
Alison Forsberg, Illustrator

Please note that Duck Light contains direct and implied references to Coraline (film) directed by Henry Selick, and The Phantom of the Opera (musical) with music by Andrew Lloyd Webber and book by Richard Stilgoe. No association is claimed, nor are any rights owned, by anyone involved in the production of Duck Light.

ISBN
978-1-03-910961-2 (Hardcover)
978-1-03-910960-5 (Paperback)
978-1-03-910962-9 (eBook)

1. FICTION, SHORT STORIES (SINGLE AUTHOR)

Distributed to the trade by The Ingram Book Company

DUCK
LIGHT

1/10
My Full Name

Lulu, the refined and worldly duck, dipped her feet into the bathtub cautiously, making sure the water was exactly the right temperature. Once she determined the water to be perfectly lukewarm, she flopped her entire body over the side of the tub and into the water, causing a flood to spill onto the floor. She placed a rubber duck toy into the water. The duck was positioned upright, but once she let go of the toy, it rolled heavily onto its side, floating as if it was lying on a bed. Next, Lulu required music to keep her occupied while in the bath. The small music player was set up on the closed lid of the toilet that was next to the tub and the sweet sound of classical music filled the room with the press of a button. Offenbach's can-can—her favourite.

Perhaps a cigarette would add to the ambience. Yes, a cigarette indeed. After lighting one up, Lulu was able to sink down into the water and relax. She sighed a deep, heavy sigh and took a drag. Her lungs felt full, yet her body felt relaxed. The first drag made her cough, but it always felt better the second time. Her eyes closed in pleasure and, with her free hand, she rubbed down the back of her head. There couldn't be a better way to relax. A bath, Offenbach, and a cigarette was all Lulu needed to clear her head. A sprinkle of ashes fell into the water. Quickly they were encased in a large, soapy bubble and then disappeared from sight.

Lulu's fiancée was in the room directly across from the bathroom. Her name was Rosie, and she was relaxing in her own way. While Lulu bathed, Rosie, across the way, worked on a 1,000-piece puzzle. After nearing ten minutes without finding a piece to place in, Rosie decided to cross the hall and visit Lulu. Six years together meant she would not need to knock on the bathroom door. She could simply enter. She had seen Lulu naked before. They were engaged. If Rosie wanted to see Lulu lying in a bathtub, societal laws permitted her to do so. So, she walked into the bathroom unannounced.

"Jesus Christ, Rosie," said Lulu.

"Thank you for calling me by my full name," replied Rosie.

Rosie leaned over the side of the bathtub to get a better look at Lulu, but became distracted when she saw the little rubber duck lying sideways in the water as if it were drowning. She placed it back upright only for it to fall back to how it had been. This time, it turned and lay on its front with its face in the water. Rosie frowned, and then smiled.

"Don't you think this duck looks like me?" she asked playfully.

"I think it looks more like me," replied Lulu.

Then, something unexpected happened. Very early on in their relationship, Lulu had given Rosie a cigarette to try. She had claimed she had never smoked before. Rosie smoked it with ease as if she was a seasoned smoker, but then insisted that she didn't like it and said she would never smoke again. She expressed her support of Lulu's habit, but said she wouldn't get in on it herself. Yet there, with her fiancée in the tub taking another long drag, Rosie had another suggestion.

"You want to try something else?" Rosie quavered.

"Like what?" Lulu answered the question with another question.

Then, out of the left breast pocket on her jean vest, Rosie pulled out a crumbly, misshapen brown object. She passed it over to Lulu. Lulu squeezed it, and bits of it fell off, crumbling into the bath. Within moments, she recognized the strange object as a brownie. How strange it was that her fiancée was carrying a brownie around in her jean vest. There are certain places you can store a brownie if you want to save it for later, but the left breast pocket of a jean vest definitely isn't one of them. Appalled, Lulu handed the brownie, which was now wet, back to her fiancée. Rosie quacked with laughter at this. She took the brownie back and tossed it in the trash bin behind her.

"I have more," tempted Rosie.

"More what?"

"More of these brownies. A whole bunch of them. I bought them today."

"You bought them? From where? And why the hell did you keep one in that dirty pocket?"

None of these questions were answered. In response, Rosie left the room, presumably to go get more brownies. When she returned, she was holding another brownie, but this one was not like the last. This brownie wasn't a crumbly ball. This brownie looked perfect. Rosie split it in half, destroying its perfect appearance. She offered one half to Lulu, who took it without a second thought. She chewed the brownie slowly, trying to savour each moment. It was perfect after all. It was moist and fudgy. After swallowing, Lulu went to ask for another but was cut off just as she opened her mouth.

"They're special brownies," said Rosie.

Special brownies! Of course they were special! They were perfect and delicious! What a great word to describe them!

Rosie caught on that Lulu had not caught on.

"Special brownies. Happy brownies. There's a million terms for them. They're the ones that have weed in them."

Lulu had smoked cigarettes for years but had never tried anything outside of cigarettes and alcohol. She had never dabbled in drugs and never had any clue that Rosie had either. Rosie didn't even smoke, and yet here she was with special brownies, the special part being marijuana. Cannabis. Weed. It was too late to go back. She had already swallowed. It was already in her system. Rosie, sensing Lulu's unease, reassured her.

"They'll help you relax."

Lulu put out her cigarette in the water and threw it toward the trash, missing only by a couple inches.

"If you say so," she sighed.

***

Not five minutes later and Lulu felt the special effect of the special brownie. First she got real dizzy, then she got euphoric. It was like she had left her body and her spirit was flying, even though she was still on the ground. It was a wonderful feeling. She expressed this to Rosie, who simply smiled and nodded.

Lulu was not in the bath anymore. She didn't remember getting out of the bath but there she was in the living room. She danced with the houseplants, the foxtails and lily pads. She tripped and fell but felt nothing as she landed. She laughed but couldn't hear herself laughing. Oh, it was wonderful.

"Rosie! Join me!" begged Lulu.

"I will. I will," promised Rosie.

Lulu was dizzy and light. She was floating. She was flying. It was like being drunk except she wasn't stupid, she was just happy. Then it stopped. She came back to earth and felt the cold floor underneath her. She realized then that she was lying on the floor and not floating above it. Still, she felt calm. She was at peace. She was in such a relaxed state that taking a bath would never come close to what she was feeling now. She lay on the hard floor. She closed her eyes. She began to hum a song. The can-can by Offenbach—her favourite. Suddenly, she wasn't alone in humming; she could hear the entire symphony in her head playing along with her.

She was the soloist and the orchestra was her accompaniment. The audience clapped and cheered and teared up. They would go home and tell their families that they had never heard such beautiful music. She was flying again.

Then she was on the floor. Then she was flying. It continued like this for a good while. She would be flying and then become aware of herself and find herself back on the floor. And then, she would again be flying. It was like a switch that she didn't control, but she didn't mind. Rosie watched all of this completely amused. She took a large bite out of her brownie and laughed deeply with her mouth full. After she finished that brownie, she had another. Lulu, having eaten only half of one, was out of her mind.

Rosie continued to watch Lulu dance and hum. Rosie ate more and more brownies, seemingly completely unaffected.

"Rosie! I've never been so happy!"

Lulu fell back down onto the floor and waited to fly again. She waited to float off the floor and rejoin the symphony. She waited. And waited. But the euphoria had slowly melted away. Now, Lulu felt extremely paranoid. Her vision blurred and the world seemed a little dimmer. It was cold, and she was afraid. She thought back to when she was flying but it seemed like such a distant memory that she thought she would never be able to fly again. She was so frightened now that she trembled. Her eyes darted around anxiously, searching for a lurking monster or hidden dangers. She looked back to where Rosie had been sitting, but she was gone.

Rosie! Rosie was gone! The lurking monster and hidden dangers had taken her away! Terrible things were going to happen to Rosie and then those same terrible things would happen to her, too! She heard the low growl of the monster that she couldn't see but she knew was close. Too scared to move, Lulu tried to take cover right where she was. Then her fear got the best of her. She began to cry. Loud sobs took over her and she waited in terror for her impending death. This was it. This was the end. And she would never see her fiancée again. Her eyes were hidden by her wings, which were now slippery with tears. She shook violently and screamed out to the cruel world that was about to take her away. And Rosie! What had happened to her? Something unspeakable! And without even a chance to say goodbye! Oh, how awful!

She cried and screamed and trembled, waiting for the end. A figure leaned over her. It was the monster! It leaned closer and closer, ready to kill and—

"Lulu. Dude. Hey. Calm down."

Was the monster really telling her to calm down before killing her?

"Lulu! Come on. It's me."

Who's 'me'?

"Lulu!" said Rosie's voice.

Rosie. Rosie! It was her!

"Rosie!" cried Lulu, "It was terrible! I was flying and then I was falling and there was this terrible monster!" She broke into more sobs.

"No, there wasn't. You're fine," said Rosie.

"It was the brownies," said Lulu in realization.

"Yeah. It was the brownies."

"None of that actually happened."

"Right."

"It was the weed. I'm never doing that again."

Rosie groaned and laughed, somehow at the same time. Puzzled, Lulu asked Rosie what was the matter.

"There was no weed," informed Rosie. "Those were just regular brownies. God, you're a fool. Now get up. Go empty the bath water."

Lulu did as told. She got up and made her way over to the bath. Before Lulu pulled the plug, Rosie said one more thing.

"By the way," she said, "your reaction was extremely exaggerated. You had half a brownie. That's nowhere near what happens when you eat half a special brownie. You're a moron. Jesus."

Lulu was embarrassed. She reached down and pulled the plug, still trying to piece together what had just happened. Her brain felt like Rosie's 1,000-piece puzzle in the other room.

***

The two lay in bed together later that night.

"Rosie, remember what you said earlier? About how my reaction was exaggerated? And that's not what really happens?"

"Yeah?"

"How would you know?"

The light in the room went off.

"Goodnight, Lulu," replied Rosie.

2/10
Margaret

Their neighbour was a squirrel. She was a rowdy thing. Margaret was her name. She did what Lulu called "squirrel stuff." Lulu once went over to her house to ask for a cup of sugar but all Margaret could pull out were various nuts and the occasional pine cone. She clearly wasn't living a life as civilized or sophisticated as Lulu and Rosie. She didn't even have a car. She got everywhere she needed to go on squirrelly feet. Mostly the only places she ever went were up high in trees and she would run at the trunk full force then somehow run up a ninety-degree

13

angle to end up at the top of a tree. What a barbarian. What an animal. What a squirrel.

One day, Margaret knocked on the door of Lulu's house. She needed help. She wanted to reach a beehive that was attached to the roof of another neighbour's shed to get some honeycomb, but she couldn't run up the siding of the shed. If only she could travel by air. If only she could fly like a duck.

"Ask someone else," said Lulu.

So Margaret carried on her way. She asked a flock of birds for help but they all chose to ignore her pleas. Margaret was upset and lonely. She was never going to reach the honeycomb. She spent days watching that shed. The bees and the birds flew up to the beehive and took all the honeycomb they wanted, but a squirrel had no way of getting up there. She couldn't climb up siding. She could only climb up trees.

Trees. That was it! She could climb trees!

All she had to do was climb up a nearby tree and then jump to the beehive. It was genius. It was foolproof. So, she did. She ran at the trunk of the tree full force and then up the tree. All of this while Lulu sat at her window and watched. What. An. Animal.

Lulu, like the civilized being that she was, poured herself a cup of tea, added a touch of Baileys, and made a nest of pillows to sit in while she watched her crazy barbarian of a neighbour try to reach the shed roof. She watched as Margaret gulped down her anxiety and prepared herself to make the jump. She watched Margaret anxiously lean forward like she was about to leap, and then lean back, and then forward, and then back. Lulu could see that Margaret was afraid, and Lulu smiled. Was there anything better than seeing someone you hate in distress? Not for Lulu there wasn't. She sipped her tea and Baileys and continued to watch this scene unfold. Finally, Margaret jumped.

She didn't reach the shed. Well, actually, she did. But barely. She reached her little squirrel hands out and then smashed her little squirrel head right into the corner of the shed's roof. There was blood, lots of it. And when Margaret hit the ground, she didn't get up. With her arms stretched out in front of her and her face in the dirt, Margaret lay there. Lulu nearly choked on her drink and had to spit some of it out, coughing. Margaret looked dead for sure. There, in her right next-door neighbour's yard was her left next-door neighbour, dead.

To be quite honest, Lulu was not fond of her right next-door neighbour. He was big and loud and mean. Lulu was scared of him and avoided him at all costs. But now, there was a dead body in his yard, and she had just witnessed the death. She couldn't just go on with her day drinking her tea as if none of it happened. What she had just seen was gruesome and over-the-top disturbing, even if Margaret was someone she hated. She had to go over to his house; she knew it. She had to knock on his door and explain to him what had happened. That's all she had to do, right? He'd take care of the rest.

Lulu left her house, comfort tea in hand, and walked over to her right next-door neighbour's house. She gulped as she had seen Margaret do earlier, and then she knocked on the door. Two knocks was all it took. He opened the door and stared down at Lulu. He smelled like what she was drinking if it had no tea in it and was only Baileys.

"Good evening, sir," Lulu stuttered, in the middle of the afternoon. "I don't mean to bother you, sir, but, sir, I was just looking out my window, sir, and there appears to be, sir, a dead squirrel in your yard, sir."

The man groaned and reached for something out of view of the doorway. Lulu watched, frightened, as the man revealed what he was reaching for and a huge, hard broom came into view.

"Get!" he shouted. "Get away!" And he pushed the broom in her direction, aiming for her feet. Lulu cried out in surprise and hightailed it back to her house. She panted heavily as she slammed the door and locked it. Exhausted from shock, she slunk down to the floor. She tried to take a sip of her tea and then realized she had lost it outside in her panic. This was going from bad to worse.

She didn't want to take another look outside but she knew she had to. There, outside the window, clear as day, was Margaret's dead body in the dirt of her scary and mean neighbour's yard. How fitting it was that her annoying and bothersome neighbour was the one that had put her in this situation with her scary and mean neighbour. No one else but Margaret would put this on Lulu. Lulu grabbed another cup and poured another shot of Baileys into it. She considered remaking a tea but slammed the shot before she could. It tasted how her neighbour smelled, and she gagged.

Something outside Lulu's window caught her eye; she turned to inspect the scene. There, in the dirt, Margaret's dead body was getting up. *Oh,* thought Lulu, both relieved and disappointed, *she isn't dead.* Margaret wiped some blood off her face and looked up longingly at the beehive and the honeycomb. Lulu could see the dismay written on Margaret's face as she moped away from the sweet prize. Lulu again knew what she had to do, and slipped quietly out her back door to go and help Margaret reach it.

3/10
Parmesan Cheese

Lulu was preparing a dinner for herself and
Rosie. The trouble was that Lulu was not a
very skilled chef. Sure, she could make good
toast, but that was about it. Tonight, she was preparing a pasta dish. Not even entirely sure how
to cook pasta, Lulu read the instructions from a
cookbook. The book was one she had found at a
small book shop in the town. She had collected
some graphic novels as well but the thought of
making recipes out of this cookbook excited her.
*A Guide to Making Food That Doesn't Taste Like
Literal Shit*, the book was called. Not only did

the recipes intrigue her, but it was the vulgar language that really caught her eye. Whoever wrote this book used the same kind of language Lulu did in her head. Though she didn't often swear out loud, she swore a lot in her thoughts. She opened the book and prepared to cook pasta for the first time in her life.

First you boil the water until it's hot as fuck. Don't forget to salt the shit out of the water while it's boiling.

Okay, this cookbook looked promising. Lulu dug through her kitchen to find a sizable pot. She felt a little confused about the water, though. She wasn't sure if it meant tap water or natural water, like from the pond outside. After considering the target audience of the book, she poured enough tap water into the pot, then placed the pot onto the stove. Now, how was she supposed to know when the water was boiled? Was she supposed to feel the water and tell by the severity of the burns it gave her? The cookbook didn't say anything about that. It skipped over a crucial part.

"Rosie!" called Lulu. "How am I supposed to tell when the water is boiled?"

"When it's bubbling!" Rosie called back.

Lulu pulled up a stool and stared at the water. It didn't appear to be bubbling yet but she didn't want to miss it when it did. She had never focused on anything so hard in her life.

Once the water is boiling, pour those little motherfuckers into it and turn down the heat. Set the timer to ten goddamn minutes and stir occasionally.

All right, easy enough. The water was now bubbling so, as instructed by the book, she poured those little motherfuckers into the water, assuming the motherfuckers in the book meant the pieces of bow-shaped pasta. Was each bow one motherfucker? After dumping those motherfuckers into the pot, she again watched intently. Now, how was she supposed to know when the pasta was ready? She could tell when the water was boiling just by looking at it but she wouldn't be able to tell the firmness of the bows using only her eyes.

"Rosie!" called Lulu again. "How do I know when the pasta is ready?"

"When the timer goes!" Rosie called back.

Oh. That would make sense. The timer for ten minutes was going to beep after the ten minutes were up, and that would indicate that the pasta was ready. She read on in the book.

Now that the pasta is done cooking, strain that shit.

Lulu dug around to find a colander to strain the pasta. When she poured the contents of the pot into the colander, the steam rose into her face.

"Pasta's done!" called Lulu.

"Make a sauce for it now!" Rosie called back.

Right. The sauce. Maybe it would say something about making a sauce in her cookbook. She flipped a page.

First you're going to need a big-ass saucepan to melt the butter. Add some garlic and stir in some fucking flour. Add in some gross-ass milk and stir the shit out of it.

Lulu did as instructed. She had to reread the steps over and over until they made some sense to her. Finally, she had completed that bit of the sauce making, but there was more to go.

Put some salt and pepper and tomato paste in there so it tastes good as fuck. Stir it around then dump that shit onto your pasta. Add some parmesan cheese if you're a classy motherfucker.

Lulu thought of herself as a classy mother-fucker, so she elegantly sprinkled parmesan on top. She shouted to Rosie to tell her that the supper was all prepared and smiled proudly. Rosie waddled up the stairs and into the kitchen. Lulu poured a glass of white wine for herself, and a glass for her fiancée, and marvelled at the piece of culinary art she had created. Rosie didn't seem to share in the excitement. Thoughtlessly, Rosie dished up and then took her plate back down-stairs and sat herself right in front of the televi-sion. Offended, Lulu took her plate over to the kitchen table. She lit a few candles, put Offenbach on, and sat down to have a nice dinner by herself.

Lulu had had several bites before she decided to scratch the nice dinner and just take her food downstairs to join Rosie at the television. Rosie was watching a movie about people with button eyes and a talking black cat. Spooky.

"What are you watching?" asked Lulu.

"Yes," replied Rosie.

Obviously Rosie was not paying any atten-tion to Lulu. With eyes locked on the TV screen, Rosie shovelled down the last bit of her pasta and pushed her plate to the side.

"Did you like the pasta?" asked Lulu.

"Coraline," replied Rosie.

Feeling rather insulted, Lulu grabbed the two empty plates and went back upstairs to wash the dishes and clean up the kitchen with no help from her fiancée. As she was putting away the cookbook, an idea came to mind. There had to be dessert recipes in there, right? She could whip up a delicious dessert and eat it all herself to spite Rosie. With a few page flips, Lulu came across a no-bake dessert section. That should be easy enough. The one that especially caught her eye was the raspberry crumble. After setting up her supplies, she began reading the recipe instructions.

You'll need to get some walnuts, dates, dried coconut, sea salt, and a whole lot of those little raspberry fucks. First thing you need to do is let them raspberries rinse under some water and then let them dry out.

So, Lulu took a handful of raspberries outside and held them under the water in the pond.

4/10
Duck Light

Lulu's big concert was coming up. She had been practising for weeks. She would be singing to a large audience and wanted desperately to impress them. The pieces she would be performing were mostly originals by her, yet she was influenced by other classical composers. For the most part, she wasn't too nervous about performing. The only part that freaked her out was the high B flat she had to hit. Often when she went to sing that high note, she would miss it by nearly a major third. It was a sour note. It didn't come easily to Lulu.

She began her last practice session before the big concert. Her main focus was that one note. She knew all the words without needing the sheet music and she knew her pieces well. It was just that one high B flat that gave her trouble. Clearing her throat first, she began to sing. The first piece she wanted to practise started in a lower register and that was fine, but as the song went on, the melody line would rise in octaves. Progressively through the song, her register became higher and higher until it eventually reached the high B flat. The notes came out of Lulu deep from her throat, and with a slight vibrato, she sang over the low register with such ease that she could fool a non-musician into thinking she had performed with all the great opera singers of the world. All was going well until the measure before the high B flat. Her nerves got the best of her and when she went to hit the note, her voice died out and, with a loud QUACK, she absolutely butchered the B flat, missing it by nearly a major sixth. Unknown to her, Margaret had been listening to Lulu practise. Margaret heard Lulu butcher that high B flat. Startled, Margaret nearly fell off the roof of Lulu's house where she had been hiding.

Lulu then noticed the squirrel, not knowing if she should feel embarrassed or angry.

"Margaret, get out of here," Lulu threatened.

Margaret made a few squirrel-like squeaks and chirps and bolted out of her hiding spot. Down the side of the house she scrambled, landing on the grass. From there, she raced full force up the side of the tree in a very squirrel-like manner and Lulu groaned, annoyed. Why couldn't she be more human, like a duck?

Lulu continued to practise. Her beak formed an O shape and the sound escaped. It was beautiful, and surely anyone who heard it would tear up. Surely they would sob over the beauty of Lulu's voice and make her go famously down in history, like Maureen Forrester. God, could anything ever sound so angelic? It was going all so well. She nailed the tricky rhythms and killed the staccato notes. But then, the high B flat.

"QUACK!" exclaimed Lulu.

With only days left until the performance, she was quickly running out of time to nail the note, and hold it for twelve beats. Poor Lulu wanted to cry.

Rosie came up from downstairs with a beer in hand. "Practising?" she asked.

"Oh, Rosie," said Lulu, "it's awful! I can't hit that note for the life of me."

Rosie held her can out as an offering to Lulu to have some beer. Duck Light. Deliciously refreshing. Lulu grabbed the can and nearly downed the drink.

"Jesus," said Rosie.

"What will I do?" Lulu asked. "The concert is in two days!"

"Let me see the music," said Rosie.

Rosie could read music, as well. Both the ducks were musically adept, though Lulu liked to think she was better. Because she so often listened to Offenbach, she liked to believe she knew more than her partner did. She liked to believe that if the two ever sang a duet, Lulu would outshine Rosie. Rosie stared at the sheet of music and made an "uh-huh" sound. She studied it purposefully.

"Give me the starting pitch," said Rosie, and Lulu hummed the starting F sharp.

With that, Rosie began to sing. She soared through the melodic line and her voice dropped with ease to the low notes. The high B flat was fast approaching. *She'll never hit it,* thought Lulu.

And then, in a surreal moment, there was a loud and long-held "OH" and then like nothing it was over and the piece continued. Rosie had just hit the note, only a few cents sharp, but not even the musically accomplished Lulu had noticed. Lulu's mouth dropped open in shock and jealousy.

The piece ended and Rosie stopped singing. Lulu was too shocked and jealous to clap.

"What part were you having trouble with?" questioned Rosie. Lulu pointed to the highest note on the page.

"Oh, you mean this one?" asked Rosie, immediately singing the note again.

"Maybe it should just be *your* concert," said Lulu.

"Well," suggested Rosie, "what if it is? I mean, just for this song?"

Lulu looked puzzled.

"Think about it!" said Rosie, "We wear the same clothes. After the piece before this one, you walk offstage to supposedly drink some water, only when you come back, it's not really you. It's me. I sing it, close the show, everyone claps, you hear it offstage, and, BAM. Concert finished!"

Lulu liked the idea, except for the part about the audience all clapping for Rosie instead of her. In one sense, it would get her out of the high B flat, in another, she would have to only imagine the audience crying and not be able to really witness it. But she thought that maybe that could be a good thing. Lulu grinned slyly.

"It's a deal," she said.

***

The day of the concert arrived. Lulu and Rosie were dressed identically in concert black and white. Their makeup was the same. Red lipstick was smeared on their beaks. No one would be able to tell the two partners apart. They looked exactly the same.

Lulu would start. She would sing four pieces and then Rosie would sneakily close the show with the fifth, and no one would be the wiser. The audience would think it was Lulu for the duration. Lulu's name was featured on the front page of the program. She knew this because she had made the program, and printed off dozens of copies. Nothing was said about Rosie except on the performer acknowledgement page. Lulu had thanked her fiancée for support, but there was nothing in there about Rosie performing onstage.

"Two minutes 'til showtime! Kill it," Rosie said, and then leaned in to give Lulu a kiss on the cheek.

"Don't get lipstick on me!" said Lulu, swerving to avoid the display of affection.

Lulu adjusted the bow in the feathers on her head and stepped onto the stage, her eyes shut in anticipation. She wouldn't open them until she started singing.

She peeked to adjust her place centre stage, closed her eyes, and started to sing. "Think of me. Think of me fondly," she sang, "when we've said goodbye."

She opened her eyes.

"Remember me, every so often, promise me you'll—MARGARET!" she screamed.

There was but one audience member. She proudly held up the program and waved it. Margaret was the only audience that had come for Lulu's performance. Lulu hadn't even realized that she had stopped singing. Margaret chirped back in a very squirrel-like pitch to respond. There was no reason to go on with the show. There was no reason to stay professional. Lulu tore the bow off her head and stomped on it. She exited stage left.

***

The next day, the two ducks had a fire outside their house. They were burning Lulu's concert sheet music one sheet at a time. When the two turned their backs on the fire to look at the stars, Margaret began to roast her collected nuts over the glow of the fire. Lulu turned back to the fire and noticed the squirrel immediately.

"MARGARET!" she screamed, just like the previous day at the concert.

Before running off, Margaret glanced toward the pile of sheet music that had not yet been burned. For the first time since living next to the squirrel, Lulu heard Margaret make a sound that was not squirrel-like at all. There was a loud and long-held "OH" as the mere squirrel hit the high B flat as easily as Rosie had. And with that, she gathered her nuts and bolted away. Lulu shredded the piece of music before tossing it into the fire.

5/10
A Family of Cacti

On a sunny Tuesday afternoon, Lulu decided she wanted a pet. She ran the idea by Rosie, who was not totally on board.

"How about a dog?" asked Lulu. "Like all the humans have."

"How about a pet rock?" replied Rosie.

Acquiring a pet was going to be difficult. It had to be a manageable size for a duck and not too messy or smelly. And of course, not be too loud or aggressive, not eat too much, not need to go on walks, not need baths or its litter box cleaned, and not need to be fed more than once a day.

Lulu was beginning to think her standards were too high.

"Maybe a mouse?" suggested Lulu.

"We could adopt a nice family of cacti," Rosie suggested back.

"How about a hedgehog?"

"How about a Chia Pet in the shape of a hedgehog?"

Lulu snuffed. Convincing Rosie was going to be a challenge. There was no way they would both agree, so maybe they would have to meet in the middle. Lulu didn't want a rock, a cactus, or a Chia Pet.

"I have an idea," said Rosie. "I'll go into town and I'll buy you a virtual pet."

Lulu beamed at the idea. A virtual pet would not be too messy or smelly. It would not be too loud or too aggressive. It wouldn't eat too much, wouldn't need walks, wouldn't need baths or its litter box cleaned. And it wouldn't have to be fed more than once a day. The idea was the perfect compromise between the two ducks. Rosie pulled her wallet out of her drawer, and then pulled out the credit card. She'd need that. That's what the humans used.

"I'll go right now," said Rosie. Lulu would wait in excited anticipation.

***

Rosie waddled into the toy store and went up to the front counter. "One virtual pet, please," she declared proudly. The human working obviously didn't understand what she had said, so Rosie said it again. And again. The human didn't move.

"A . . . alright," said Rosie, "I'll go pick one myself." She waddled off.

The selection of virtual pets was small but she only needed one anyway. The little electronic devices came in a variety of colours and shapes. Each had an "on" button, a "feed" button, and a "clean" button. The pets looked like little computer graphic blobs with small dotted eyes and thin lines for mouths. Some had cute ears, similar to those of a cat, some had interesting hair atop their heads, some had multiple legs, and some were just round faces. Rosie picked one of the round ones and carried it back to the counter. Someone was ahead of her in line, so she waited patiently—until she heard the human's voice. She recognized it instantly. It was her scary right next-door neighbour. What was he buying? He didn't have kids.

There was a sound from Rosie's feathery wing, where she was clutching the virtual pet. She had accidentally turned it on, and it began to beep, indicating that the pet was hungry.

"Quiet down!" Rosie commanded. It continued to beep.

The neighbour turned around. There, he saw it. A duck holding onto a virtual pet toy. He looked puzzled, but Rosie read it as anger and flew out as fast as she could. She didn't pay for the toy, so more beeping ensued as the store's security system recognized it as a stolen item. Shouting could be heard behind her. Her adrenaline pumping, Rosie scrambled back to the river with the beeping toy. The river would take her to a pond, which would take her to her house, where she could give the round virtual being to her partner. She crashed into the river, making sure the toy didn't get wet, and let the flowing water carry her downstream. She had made it safely out of the toy store and away from her scary right next-door neighbour.

When she reached the pond, Lulu was waving over by the house. She had a huge grin spread across her duckbill. She was excited for the toy. Rosie kicked her webbed duck feet and swam over to her, toy in hand. It was still beeping. She handed it off to its new owner.

"Why does it beep?" asked Lulu.

"On the package it says it beeps when it's hungry," replied Rosie. Lulu pressed the "feed" button.

Small dots sprinkled down from the top of the screen and the pet opened its mouth like a yawning hamster and gobbled up the food. "Mmmmm!" said the virtual pet.

"What will you name it?" Rosie wanted to know.

"I think he should be called Eddie," replied Lulu.

So Eddie was home, and part of the family. Lulu giggled in delight and brought Eddie inside, where she began to show him around the house. Rosie thought this was weird.

Lulu played all day with Eddie. She fed him over and over again, and cleaned up after him, and talked to him as if he were a real pet. "You're a good boy," she would tell him. Eddie beeped in agreement.

When it was time for the ducks to head to bed, Lulu made Eddie his own bed out of a small cardboard box and a scrap piece of fabric. She tenderly set the bed beside her own bed and whispered good night to her new pet. Rosie thought this, too, was weird. But, Eddie was part of the family now, and that had to be accepted.

There was a beeping in the night—only this time, Eddie was not hungry. His battery was close to dying. If Lulu didn't get a replacement battery soon, Eddie would die, and she would be a murderer. She was reminded of that time Margaret supposedly died in her right next-door neighbour's yard and the panic that had caused. This was the same.

"Shut that damn thing up," said Rosie.

Lulu flew out of bed in search of a battery. She had the screwdriver to unscrew the back of the toy, but no fresh battery to put in. Batteries were more of a human thing.

A human thing! That's it! Her right next-door neighbour was a human! He'd have a battery!

"I have to save Eddie," said Lulu, grabbing her coat.

"Whatever," replied Rosie.

Lulu slipped Eddie into her coat pocket and crept out the door. She knew she had to get into her right next-door neighbour's house without being seen or heard. She knew how angry the scary man would be to see a duck in his house in the night. She knew he wasn't particularly fond of ducks. Once she was out of her house, she snuck over to her neighbour's, Eddie beeping like there would be no tomorrow. And, at this rate, there may not be for him.

"Wait here," Lulu told Eddie as she placed him on the grass outside the door. "Beep, beep, beep!" said Eddie.

Lulu somersaulted like a spy in a movie and sprang back up at the front door with her wing in a gun shape at her bill. Spy music played in her head. She peeked in the window and saw the scary man asleep on the couch. The TV was on, and he was clutching the remote. The remote would have a battery in it, wouldn't it? She would need to steal the remote. She was in luck—the front door was not yet locked. She tried the handle and the door swung open silently. She stepped in.

The man snored loudly. Lulu pressed her body against the wall and slid over to his couch. He snored louder and she startled, thinking she'd be caught, but he was still asleep. She reached for the remote and grabbed hold. It was not difficult to ease it out of the sleeping man's hand.

She had her prize. There was no need to be sneaky now. She dashed away, loudly knocking over a lamp and waking the man. *Shit!* she thought.

She propelled herself out the door but, in the darkness, she couldn't see Eddie. She could hear a faint beeping, but had completely lost sight of her new pet. The man was now getting up to investigate the scene. She had to get out of there! But not without Eddie! The beeps were getting softer, with longer pauses between them. He needed the battery, and he needed it now. Lulu scrambled in the grass until she felt a hard plastic object. It was Eddie!

Eddie in one hand, remote in the other, Lulu launched herself off the grass and back into her own house. She had no intention of returning the remote.

With a little help from her duckbill, she popped off the back of the remote, where a shiny battery sparkled inside. Lulu knew it would fit in Eddie's case. She replaced the battery and was greeted by a friendlier beeping. Eddie was alive once again, and he was a hungry one. Lulu laughed to herself and pressed the "feed" button. Eddie opened his mouth like a yawning hamster and gobbled up the food. "Mmmmm!" said Eddie.

6/10
The Phantom of
the Duck Pond

The two ducks were in bed one night when Lulu was startled awake by a dream. She was not fully asleep, but half asleep, and in her dream, she was falling. She jolted awake and her eyes popped open wide in fear. Rosie too was startled by seeing this and asked her partner why she had suddenly awoken so abruptly.

"I almost died," said Lulu.

"Good thing you didn't. You know what happens when you die?" said Rosie.

"What?" Lulu asked nervously.

"You become a wandering ghost. Stuck in this dimension for all eternity. Hopelessly wandering around the space you died in. Forever."

Now this startled Lulu even more. *Ghosts?* Now *that* was a scary thought.

"Rosie?" said Lulu. "You don't think perhaps it was a ghost that woke me out of my sleep?"

"Well, in fact," replied Rosie, "it probably was."

Rosie was just teasing, but Lulu was easily scared. Rosie recalled the time with the brownie and how easily Lulu had been convinced that there were lurking monsters out to get her. Scaring her partner was sort of fun, in a way. Lulu was in no real danger so it seemed harmless enough.

The following morning, Rosie decided to play a little mind game on Lulu. The duck was playing with her virtual pet when she left it on the couch to use the bathroom. Rosie quickly snatched the toy and hid it in another room. She giggled to herself in an evil way. This would convince Lulu there was a ghost in the house. Rosie heard the toilet flush and sneakily went back to what she was doing, leaving no evidence that she had been anywhere near the couch. Lulu paced back to the couch but stopped in her tracks after noticing it was vacant. No virtual pet anywhere.

"Hey, where's Eddie?" Lulu asked Rosie.

"Probably right where you left him," replied Rosie.

"No. He isn't there."

"Well I didn't move him. Maybe it was the ghost."

Ghost? thought Lulu. The ghost had got a hold on her beloved Eddie! Oh, it was terrible!

"Help me look for him!" cried Lulu as she desperately tore the room apart. Pillows were flying. The table was turned upside down. Eddie was nowhere to be found. Rosie sat back and sipped her tea, laughing at the chaos.

Lulu raced into the kitchen, where Rosie was sitting and Eddie was hidden. In fact, he wasn't even really hidden. He was just on the counter. After tearing apart the second room, Lulu spotted him. The ghost had moved Eddie from the couch to the kitchen. What else would the phantom do?

***

The ghost was relatively inactive for the rest of the day, but things got worse a couple days later. Lulu was convinced she could hear a spooky "Ooooooo" sound at night. Rosie knew this was just the wind outside but really played it up to be the ghost. She pretended to be frightened as well. One night, the two ducks were in bed and the "Ooooooo" was loudly howling. Rosie decided to ramp up the mind games. She would quietly whisper Lulu's name in a raspy voice unrecognizable as her own. Lulu damn near pissed herself every time. She pulled the covers up above her duckbill so only her eyes were uncovered, darting around in fear.

Suddenly, there was a loud rap on the window.

"Rosie!" exclaimed Lulu, "Did you hear that?"

The thing is, Rosie *had* heard it. And she hadn't caused it.

Rosie, now trying to be the tough guy, scoffed at the rap. "It was probably nothing," she said.

"It was probably the ghost!" said Lulu.

Rosie's shenanigans were over. She too was now scared of the ghost. Lulu clutched Eddie to protect him from the phantom of the duck pond.

"He's there, the phantom of the duck pond," said Lulu.

"Beware, the phantom of the duck pond," replied Rosie.

The two ducks were now both completely under the covers. Then, another loud rap. Then, another. That made three loud raps on the window. Only then, Rosie started to feel silly. She had been trying to scare her partner, and now she was scared as well. Rosie peeped out of the covers and decided to go outside to check it out.

"I'm going outside," she said. Lulu only nodded.

Rosie anxiously left the comfort of the bed and tiptoed outside, so as not to alert the ghost that she was there. She crept out the back door and proceeded to the window. A gulp, and then the last few steps around the corner to the window.

Rap rap rap rap rap rap!

Retreat! Rosie bolted back in the house, breathing heavily. She collapsed onto the floor. The ghost had almost gotten her.

Now, slower. *Rap. Rap. Rap. Rap.* Rosie could hear it from the kitchen. It was loud.

Lulu bravely stepped out of the safety of the bed and into the kitchen to see Rosie. She was anxious to hear the news of the phantom. Rosie, not wanting to admit the rapping had scared her into running back inside, just shrugged her shoulders.

RAP! An even more dynamic strike hit the window and echoed through the house. Both ducks jumped in surprise. Lulu still had Eddie, who beeped in fear. Rosie suggested they get back in bed. Truthfully, she now just wanted to hide under the covers in safety. So, Lulu, Eddie, and Rosie all climbed back into the comfort of their bed. The rapping continued.

Eventually, the ducks, though petrified, fell asleep. When they awoke the next morning, the sun's bright light came in through the window. Nothing was as scary in the daytime. Lulu stepped out of bed to make a breakfast out of her cookbook for Rosie. Rosie decided to stay in bed just a little longer.

Lulu read the book. *Get some fucking flour, salt, sugar, and baking powder. Mix that shit in a bowl. Now, find another fucking bowl and beat the shit out of those little egg fuckers. Stir in milk, vanilla, and butter. Oh, and pour some 2 percent–ass milk in there, too. Hopefully you've preheated your waffle iron. Stir up your batter and slowly ladle that shit into the motherfucking waffle iron.*

RAP!

Oh no. The ghost had not gone away. Rosie yelled from bed. Lulu abandoned her waffles. Eddie beeped. However, the fears of the night had dissipated in the light of day, and Lulu, for once, felt brave.

"I'm going out there," Lulu called to her partner. "I'm going to find the ghost."

Out she went. She left Eddie inside with the burnt waffles, and Rosie in bed. She crept out sneakily, not wanting to startle an angry ghost. She reminded herself of the bravery it had taken to save her beloved Eddie, and channelled that same bravery now.

There, perched on the ledge of the window, Lulu found a woodpecker, pecking at the window. *Rap rap rap,* it went.

7/10
Cordially Invited

A six-pack of Duck Light tempted Lulu in the fridge. Rosie was sick with an unknown virus that had left her with a sore throat, high temperature, and a lot of dry coughing. Lulu had been taking care of her all day and needed to relax. She grabbed a can of Duck Light and proceeded to shotgun the beer like a high schooler at a bush party. She tossed the can and promptly grabbed another. Then she proceeded to do the same thing.

Lulu waddled into the bedroom, where her partner was sprawled out on the bed, too warm for the covers.

"Maybe you're sick with that human virus," Lulu said, "you know, the one the humans are all up in arms about."

"I don't have that one," Rosie coughed back. "I haven't touched my face at all."

The humans were all locked in their houses, and schools closed months earlier than they were supposed to. Grocery store shelves were bare. Air spaces were closed to foreign aircrafts. It was like the damn apocalypse out in the human world. Lulu had been carefully following the news and knew all of what was happening. The news urged all humans to stay on top of washing their hands and to refrain from touching their faces. Masks were suggested, but nothing was ever said of masks made to fit a duck. Lulu, of course, did the same as the humans, just without the mask part. Ducks were as close to humans as animals could get, but their face shape was quite significantly different.

Lulu wasn't so sure that Rosie didn't have the virus. Her symptoms all matched up. However,

Lulu wasn't sure what to do next. So her partner has the human virus, now what? What was she to do? Surely no human hospital would take a duck.

"I'm going to go find a newspaper," said Lulu. "I'm going to read about what to do when your partner has the human virus."

"It's like you don't even hear me when I talk," Rosie coughed again. "I don't have your stupid virus."

The closest place that may have a free newspaper stand was the local library. Lulu threw on some shoes and headed out to the library. It was a bit of a walk, but she could make it.

The streets were dead. No cars. No dogs walking. Nothing. As she passed by parking lots, she noticed the lack of parked cars. The humans were all barricaded in their houses with twenty packages of pasta and too many rolls of toilet paper to count. Lulu took this quiet opportunity to sing to herself as she walked. "Passing bells, and sculpted angels, cold and monumental . . ." she sang.

Once she reached the library, she waddled right up to the automatic doors. But they didn't open. She gazed up to human eye level and noticed a large red sign. "SORRY," it read. "WE ARE CLOSED TO THE PUBLIC. ONLY STAFF ARE PERMITTED IN THE LIBRARY UNTIL FURTHER NOTICE."

It didn't even say, "Sorry for any inconvenience." It just plainly said, "Sorry." How rude.

Lulu peered inside and saw the stand of free newspapers, but she couldn't get to them. Suddenly, a car pulled up to the library. A woman wearing a tag on a lanyard approached the doors and retrieved her cell phone from her purse. "Hey, I'm outside," she said into the phone. Lulu watched as a security worker approached the doors and opened them from the inside. The woman walked right in, and Lulu walked right behind her, matching her pace and footsteps.

Of course, the humans noticed the small duck and went to shoo her away, but not before she snatched a newspaper. The security worker kicked at the duck as she fled, but she held on to the newspaper. She strolled back home with it tucked under her wing.

At home, Lulu opened the paper and spread it across the bed, where Rosie was still sprawled. She scanned the headlines looking for anything human virus–related that may tell her how to take care of an infected loved one. She didn't have to look very hard. The entire paper was based around the virus.

"It says here," said Lulu, "that you should self-isolate for at least two weeks."

"I guess we're in quarantine now," Rosie coughed.

"What will we do?" asked Lulu. "We'll be so bored if we can't go out."

"Oh, boohoo," Rosie coughed, sarcastically. "Why don't you write a book about your woes?"

Only then, something happened. It was then, at that very moment, that Lulu coughed. Dear God, she had caught the virus.

"It is airborne, isn't it?" Rosie coughed.

"I thought you said you didn't have it," Lulu coughed back.

And so, both ducks lay sprawled out on the bed, too warm for the covers. They were in quarantine together.

***

Two days into quarantine, Lulu couldn't take it anymore. She was bored out of her head.

She needed stimulation. She needed to go out. She was still feeling under the weather, but not enough that she needed to stay in bed all day everyday like her woebegone partner was doing. However, to keep the virus from spreading, she was forced into quarantine. All the newspapers said it. There were older ducks that lived nearby that could easily have a much more severe reaction to the human virus if they caught it. The elderly were much more compromised. However, the other ducks didn't have houses like Lulu and Rosie did, so they were already more vulnerable.

"Rosie," Lulu said, "I am so bored."

Rosie turned to face her partner. Come to think of it, Lulu wasn't just her partner. They were engaged. Lulu had proposed to her a couple years ago, yet they still had no plans for a wedding. But then again, who would even come to a lesbian duck wedding?

"Well," Rosie said, not coughing, "maybe you should make wedding invitations."

"Who's getting married?" Lulu asked.

"Us!"

Oh. Right. Lulu had almost forgotten that she'd proposed. Rosie had accepted the proposal and the ring, which she couldn't even wear because she was a duck, but they had never talked of a wedding. Rosie must've been getting bored too to even bring up the topic. Wedding invitations? Who would she invite? Margaret? No, she didn't like Margaret. Her right next-door neighbour? No, he was scary. Eddie? Yes, him for sure. That woodpecker that pecked on the window? Well, maybe. Only if he wanted to come.

"Well, when is our wedding?" asked Lulu.

"You know when it gets too cold here and we vacation down south for the winter? I think we could get married then."

That was coming up soon. Some of the leaves were already starting to change colour. It was nearly hot chocolate season for the humans.

"Okay, well then, I better start on those invitations," Lulu said, grabbing another Duck Light beer to sip while she made them.

Lulu's favourite colour was pink, so obviously the invitations would be pink. She glued some fake pearls along the edges. Carefully, with her comfort grip pen, she began to write the invitations.

"YOU ARE CORDIALLY INVITED,' it read, 'TO THE WEDDING OF MISS LULU AND MISS ROSIE. WE REQUEST YOUR PRESENCE AT OUR WINTER WEDDING DOWN SOUTH."

All right, that sounded clear enough. Everyone would surely know where and when it would be. Lulu drew a little duck in a wedding dress on each invitation. She wasn't sure if it was her or Rosie, but figured it didn't matter much.

The next step was to hand out the invitations. Eddie got his early, but her plan was to take all the invitations with her when she went down south and hand them out to any other ducks vacationing. They could buy their wedding dresses down there. Oh, it would be beautiful. Suddenly, she couldn't wait.

When each and every invitation was completed, Lulu stacked them and stashed them under their bed, where Rosie was still sprawled out. She was now using the stolen free newspaper as a blanket.

"Hey," said Rosie, not coughing, "give me a sip of your beer."

Lulu passed the Duck Light over to her partner. "Are you feeling better?" she asked.

"A bit," replied Rosie.

Rosie examined the invitations. They were girly and pretty, definitely portraying the two females in the relationship. She sipped the beer and ran her feathers over the pearls. A tear almost came to her eye. She was getting married. She could hardly believe it. Soon enough, flurries would fall from above and the two lovers would go on their escapade down south, as they did together every year.

"Now what am I supposed to do for the other twelve days of quarantine?" asked Lulu.

Rosie coughed again.

8/10
And That's The Tea

After the two weeks of self-isolation were up and both ducks felt back to their normal self, Lulu and Rosie decided to go for a walk before it got too cold for ducks to be outside. Piles of leaves littered the yard and Margaret often jumped in them for some kind of deranged squirrel pleasure. Lulu enjoyed laughing at this in a sort of mocking way.

Perhaps they'd go for a swim in the pond before it froze over. They dipped their feet in and let their entire bodies be embraced by the cold water. Lulu preferred her baths, but a little swim after two weeks of isolation might do them good. They kicked their little webbed feet, and off they went. Rosie dipped her head in, searching for something to munch. *Real sophisticated*, thought Lulu, as she did the same.

All of a sudden, a tiny but intricately fragile snowflake fell onto her bill. Snowing? Already?

"We haven't even started packing!" cried Lulu.

"Relax," Rosie replied. "The first snowfall never stays long. It's still September. We've got time."

Canadian autumns were always like this. The leaves would turn a golden-brown mid-September and before they even had a chance to completely fall, it would start to snow. Lulu thought this must confuse the trees.

"It's cold. I'm going back inside," said Lulu.

"I'm enjoying my swim," her partner replied.

Lulu waddled back inside the house, where she brewed herself a warm cup of tea. No Baileys this time, just straight black tea. She shivered, and drank her tea in a massive gulp that burned her tongue and throat, but the warmth felt good. More snow fell outside and a breath of wind gently plucked some more leaves off the trees.

Perfectly, the dead leaves landed atop the piles in the yard. Margaret poked her head out of one.

Lulu watched out the window where Rosie was still paddling in the pond. The woodpecker sat perched on the windowsill. "Don't even think about it," she said. The woodpecker flew off.

Rosie decided to have a snack just fit for a duck. None of that human junk for now, just straight duck food. Her partner wasn't there to stop her. She dunked her head in the water and swiftly caught a couple of aquatic insects. As she ate them, she hoped she hadn't just ruined their date. Still hungry, and craving a tadpole, she dunked her head back in and got a mouth-ful of pond weeds. They were a staple in the diet of a regular duck, but quite honestly, they were pretty nasty. A spotted frog floated lazily past the duck. Maybe she could sneakily follow the frog and find a group of tadpoles swimming together. Surely the mother wouldn't notice if she ate just one, right?

Back inside, Lulu ate crackers and jam from the grocery store, like a human.

Rosie followed the frog slowly, as she was much faster than it was. Lulu took the opportunity to double dip her spoon into the jar of jam and lick it clean.

The frog led Rosie back to the north side of the pond, where it joined up with another frog. The two frogs then dove into the water. Rosie stuck her head in after them, hoping to catch a tadpole. A shred of guilt came over her when she rationalized eating an innocent frog's baby, but her craving was strong enough to overcome the guilt. However, she had immediately lost sight of the frog pair in the murky waters. Not a moment later, before disappointment could arrive, a small round object with a tail swam across her bill. *Tadpole!*

Rosie did manage to get the little creature in her mouth, but the slippery devil slid right out and back into the pond. This was actually lucky because when the taste of her quarry registered, she realized that her prized tadpole was just another lump of unappetizing pond weeds. Embarrassed by her absurdity, she pushed the thought of autumn tadpoles out of her mind and searched for a way to get the taste of the mushy plants out of her mouth. Perhaps a worm would do it? And she wouldn't even have to feel bad about eating a worm. They didn't even have any eyes. So, off she went, in search of a worm.

In the house, Lulu had finished off the jar of jam with a spoon.

Rosie exited the pond and decided she'd try her right next-door neighbour's garden. There must be worms in there. The garden was home to rows of vegetables that the man grew himself. However, now in the colder weather, the vegetables weren't doing so well. They were more of a May-to-August thing.

It's not very easy for ducks to dig in dirt. It's much easier for them to poke their heads in the water and catch something that way. However, the man had left a small gardening shovel in the garden, placed just perfectly for Rosie to use. She used it to her advantage and soon a worm made itself apparent. Rosie wasted no time and ate the worm. The taste of pond weeds in her mouth evolved into the delicious taste of worm. She decided to head back inside to her partner, feeling satisfied from her snacks.

When she heard the front door to the house open and then shut, Lulu quickly hid the empty jar of jam.

"How was the swim?" she asked.

Rosie didn't confess that she had just explored her duck roots. Instead, she said "Fine" and carried on.

Lulu hadn't even noticed that it had stopped snowing and the sun was shining. When Rosie pointed it out to her, her fears of not having packed yet disappeared. Now that the sun was out, it was more like a regular autumn day again. The snow on the ground had already melted away, leaving the grass wet. The piles of leaves in the yard were less-so piles now, as Margaret's playfulness had destroyed them.

"Want a cup of tea?" Lulu offered. "We have black tea, green tea, pink tea, polka-dotted tea, zebra-striped tea, neon yellow tea, rainbow tea . . ."

"Just black," replied Rosie, "and put a shot of Baileys in it."

Lulu fixed up the cup of tea and handed it to Rosie.

"So, listen," said Rosie, "I found out humans use the word 'tea' in another context."

Lulu was all ears. She loved hearing about things the humans did.

"'Tea' means, sort of drama . . . or gossip. Like 'What's the tea?' means like, 'What's the hearsay?' Or, 'That's the tea' is like 'That's the buzz.'"

Lulu was intrigued. "Give me an example," she said.

"Well, for example, you might be talking about how Margaret ruined all our leaf piles, and then you'd say, 'And that's the tea.'" To make her point clear, Rosie took a sip of her black tea.

"Where'd you learn this?"

"Well, when I was buying crackers and jam from the grocery store, there was a group of girls coming out of the liquor store saying it. I listened for a while until I got a grasp on what they really meant. I knew they couldn't have been talking about actual tea."

"What were they buying?"

"Vodka."

"And that's the tea."

Both ducks burst into laughter. Rosie nearly spilled her black tea and Baileys on herself.

***

Rosie followed up with another observation on the group of girls. She explained to Lulu about how one of them was using some kind of electronic cigarette. Lulu thought that was pretty cool and was determined to look into it and get one. Her very own electronic cigarette. It sure would come in handy on their long trip down south. But where would she get one?

"We could probably just swipe one off a human," suggested Rosie, "I'm not sure where you can get them either."

"Well, let's start by going back to the liquor store," said Lulu. Rosie nodded.

The ducks laced up their boots and headed out. Their favourite grocery store was a little less than a kilometre away and right beside it was the liquor store. That's often where they got their Baileys. But then, Rosie had a genius idea.

"We don't need to go to the liquor store!" she told Lulu. "You know how you buy your cigarettes at the little convenience store across the field? Maybe they'd have what we're looking for there."

Lulu followed up. "But we've already started walking and I didn't bring my money."

"So? We'll steal it." Now, Lulu nodded.

The ducks changed their course and started walking toward the convenience store, which was a little closer to their house than the grocery store. In front of their house was the pond, and behind their house was the field. The store where they Lulu's got cigarettes was across the field.

Once there, they headed inside. They had to walk up to the counter, as the cigarettes were behind it, and likely the electronic cigarettes were, too. The human working at the store that day was busy restocking some beef jerky and, luckily, he had his back turned to the ducks. They gazed up at the wall behind the counter, and there they saw their prize. A sign for "Vape Pens" was large and flashy, and hung on the hooks below were the electronic cigarettes. All sorts of flavours of juices were displayed, too. There was vanilla, blue raspberry, mango, mint, waffle, coffee, and more.

"Now," whispered Rosie, "just grab a pen and a juice and get out. Quickly!" Again, Lulu nodded.

They each grabbed their prized electronic cigarettes, now called "vape pens," and a bottle of flavoured juice for them. Rosie picked mint, secretly hoping for tadpole flavour. Lulu picked coffee. Lulu couldn't wait to get out of the store and try it out.

Rosie recalled the time she stole the virtual pet and the beeping to indicate a stolen item that had ensued. She desperately hoped that wouldn't happen this time. Luckily, it didn't.

As soon as the pair was outside, they unpackaged their pens to test them out. They threw the boxes in the recycling bin, as even ducks know littering is bad, and held their new pens like they were gold. Their pens were both the same model and operated in exactly the same way. It didn't take long for the pair to figure out that all they had to do was hold down the button and breathe in.

"It tastes just like real coffee!" said Lulu.

"Mine is like a candy cane," replied Rosie, thinking fondly of Christmastime.

The ducks vaped their way home. No doubt this would keep them occupied during the travel portion of their vacation down south. When they arrived back at their house, the two continued vaping until their pens had to be charged.

"They sure do die pretty quickly," said Lulu, after only an afternoon of vaping.

"And that's the tea," replied Rosie.

9/10
Migration Vacation

At the end of September and early October, Lulu and Rosie had to start planning for their migration. The other ducks at the pond were doing the same. In the past, the two had tried to travel by airplane down south for the winter but they found the humanness of the airport too confusing. What was a "boarding pass"? Grumpily, the ducks would have to once again fly using their wings like their peers. They didn't often use their wings for flying—more so like the hands of a human.

They couldn't pack up their entire house to take with them, so they had to choose only the necessities. Each duck had her own backpack she could fill with the items she wanted to bring along for the winter. Lulu had Eddie with extra batteries, cigarettes, her vape with extra juice, the cookbook, a book of sheet music, the wedding invitations, and so on. Rosie had her vape without extra juice, as she would be sharing with Lulu, a couple outfits of clothes for the hot weather, the pillow from her bed, and so on. Both ducks also had their engagement rings packed securely in the small pocket of their packs.

"You're packing much more than me," said Rosie. "How are you going to fly with that on?"

"Only the essentials," replied Lulu.

"A cookbook is an essential? Where are your clothes?"

"It'll be too hot for clothes anyway."

"So you'll be naked?"

Lulu smiled flirtatiously.

Usually all the ducks at the pond would start their migration together as a group, but this year, Lulu and Rosie were a little later to leave. Some of the other ducks had already left.

Commonly before the flock of ducks would leave, there would be a large gathering at the pond. The ducks would eat and laugh and swim before they all took off together to fly to their winter destination which would feel more like summer. Ducks hate the cold. With a passion.

It was starting to snow again. Some of the pond had already frozen over with a thin and delicate layer of ice. Lulu enjoyed walking on it to crunch it. Rosie rolled her eyes at her partner's childlike playfulness.

Both their left next-door neighbour and right next-door neighbour would be staying put for the winter. They could see how Margaret, a squirrel, would stay, but their right next-door neighbour was a human. Surely he could travel by airplane somewhere warmer for the winter, couldn't he? Whatever, they didn't care much about him and his life decisions. If he wanted to stay, they weren't going to fight him on it. As for Margaret, well, squirrels are special.

Lulu waddled around the rooms of the house, saying a temporary goodbye to each one. It would be a few months before she slept in their bed with Rosie again, or cooked in the kitchen, or took a warm bath. Rosie, too, had a bit of a hard time leaving. She said a temporary goodbye to her puzzle room and television. Maybe they would find a nice hotel down south that would house a big flat-screen television they could watch reality shows on.

"Are you almost ready?" asked Lulu, double checking she had all her important items packed.

"I guess so," Rosie sighed. This part was hard.

"Okay, say your last goodbye," Lulu said. "It's not forever, you know."

And with that, the duck pair put on their backpacks and ascended into the air. And off they went.

***

The flight was long. Several days, at least. They had to stop frequently to rest and feed. Lulu was regretting packing so much, as her backpack was weighing her down and making her body feel heavy and tired. She dared not tell Rosie, who had warned her of this. At their first rest stop, the ducks pulled down to a truck stop beside a highway. There were humans there reading maps and buying refreshing drinks to replenish themselves. The ducks did the same. Rosie had packed the map. She pulled it out as Lulu went to buy soft drinks for them, and maybe a little candy for a snack. Some red licorice sounded ideal right about now.

Rosie confirmed they were on the right track. Lulu came back with two soft drinks and a licorice string, struggling to carry it all. The two sipped their drinks and shared the long licorice string romantically. They were getting married soon, after all.

Some quacking ducks flew overhead. This also confirmed they were headed the right way. Lulu and Rosie could try to catch up with them, or they could continue to fly together, just the two of them.

"At least we don't quack obnoxiously when we fly," said Lulu. "Ugh, such ducks."

The pair decided to chug their drinks and continue on their way, when they noticed a group of truck drivers gawking and taking pictures of them. "These ducks let me get so close!" said one man. Couldn't these people just realize that the couple was just as human as them?

Lulu stretched her wings and Rosie copied her. Then, as quickly as they arrived, they took off into the air. The humans cheered from down below. One even quacked mockingly. Disgusting.

***

Their next rest stop was a pond similar to the one they lived near at home. There was already a group of ducks hanging out and resting at the pond, so Lulu decided to take the opportunity to hand out the wedding invitations. They were a little crumpled from being so tightly packed in the backpack, but they were still readable. Lulu swam up to each duck and gave every one an invitation.

"The wedding will take place once we've reached our destination," she explained to the group, "and once me and Rosie here have got our wedding dresses." She smiled proudly and the group of ducks seemed to smile back. Rosie, meanwhile, was looking for a tadpole to eat.

Rosie swam back over to her partner once Lulu had handed out the last invitation. They reckoned they would stay the night at this pond. They had to get to know their wedding attendees anyway, didn't they? There was no real bed to rest in but some of the ducks had fallen asleep floating gently on the pond and letting the water push them around. Lulu suddenly missed her house, but when she reminded herself of the snow, she was glad to be where she was. So, the pair joined the group and slept floating gently on the pond. It was a restful sleep. Just what they needed to push the extra few miles to their vacation spot.

In the morning, the ducks fed themselves with whatever they could find around the pond, and then flew off. Lulu and Rosie lagged a bit behind so they could be alone together. If they planned everything correctly, this should be the last day of their journey. By nightfall they should be down south in a nice hotel, or maybe even a tropical resort. One more day of flying would be all it took. Soon, they'd be vacationing. Soon, they'd be picking out their wedding dresses. Soon, they'd be a married couple.

The weather gradually got warmer and sunnier as they continued south. The sun beat down on their wings as they flew and Lulu could just taste the tropical margaritas she'd soon be drunk on. Within the day, they could see the flock of ducks ahead of them start to make their descent down to their destination. Lulu and Rosie continued a little farther into the city to look for wedding dress shops. Well, actually, they were looking for two different shops, so as not to spoil the surprise for each other of their wedding day looks.

"You look around here and I'll keep flying," Rosie said to Lulu, taking charge of the situation.

Lulu did as told and swooped down to get a closer look at the shops. First, she stopped into a fast food restaurant to get a hamburger and large fries, then she waddled down the street in search of a dress shop.

"Eileen's Beauty and Bridal Shop," said a sign up ahead.

Lulu quacked and jumped into the air in excitement. She waddled inside confidently, noticing a sign with the shop's hours, which said they were due to close in about half an hour. Lulu had to do this fast. In and out. She had to try on and make a decision. No time to waste.

A few blocks away, Rosie was in a jewellery shop, decking herself out in blingy bracelets and a flower corsage. The lady helping her laughed at the sight of a duck wearing her products, but stopped laughing once Rosie flew out the doors without paying for any of it. Stealing was kind of becoming her thing.

***

The two met up later in the evening, both carrying garment bags. "Where should we stay?" asked Lulu.

Rosie, on her travels, had seen a three-storey hotel with a rooftop swimming pool. She described it in exaggerated detail to her partner and they headed there together. They settled into a room and turned on the TV.

"I wonder where the other ducks are staying," said Lulu.

"Where and when did you say our wedding would be?" Rosie followed up.

"Down south once we've reached our destination."

"Sounds clear enough to me. Surely the other ducks will show up."

When it got dark enough outside, Rosie turned the TV off and unpacked the pillow from her bed. It was squished in her backpack, but it was light and hardly affected the travel. She knocked off the crummy hotel pillows and set hers in their place. Lulu snuggled in beside her.

"So our wedding is tomorrow then, isn't it? We're here." said Rosie.

"Yes, I think so." replied Lulu.

All snuggled up together in their new home for the winter, the fiancées drifted off to sleep.

DUCK LIGHT

10/10
One, Two, Three!

The big day arrived. The dresses were found. The invitations handed out. It was time to get married. Eddie was the officiant. He had a fresh battery in and beeped excitedly.

To keep from seeing each other too early, Lulu was getting ready at the hotel, and Rosie would be getting all dolled up down at the beach where they were to be married. Lulu was blushing the whole time she put her dress on.

Since Rosie was putting her gown on at the site, it was her job to set things up. They were expecting a large number of ducks to show up, so they needed many chairs. There was a white pedestal that Eddie was placed on to be the official officiant. Rosie also littered the beach with pink flowers, her partner's favourite colour.

Soon it was all set up and the duck guests started to arrive. Rosie slipped into her dress and waited at the altar for Lulu. It wasn't going to be completely like a traditional human wedding, but there were no humans in attendance, so who would even know? The other ducks wouldn't care.

Time ticked on and Lulu wasn't showing up. Rosie wasn't sure whether to feel angry or concerned.

Back at the hotel, Lulu had her dress on but was having a makeup situation. She just couldn't choose which colour to do her eyeshadow and lipstick. She wanted them to match. She couldn't do pink—that would be too expected. She couldn't do black; she didn't want to look goth. What would it be? Red? Purple? Yellow? Zebra striped?

At the beach, the ducks quacked to each other in confusion. Where was the other bride? Some even started to leave after waiting, bored, in their seats for too long. Rosie was frustrated with their lack of human-like understanding.

"Wait! Don't go!" cried Rosie, "She'll be here any second now!"

The ducks all stared at her, waiting for something to happen.

"Uh, what did the zero say to the eight?" she said into the empty eyes of the staring ducks.

There was no sound. Rosie just about forgot the rest of the joke.

"Um . . . 'Nice belt!'" she followed up, finishing her joke. Some of the ducks quacked. She didn't know if they were laughing at her joke, or at her.

Suddenly, Lulu, wearing silver eyeshadow and lipstick to accentuate her white dress, appeared at the top of the aisle. Slowly, she approached her bride, leaving webbed footprints in the sand as she walked. The wedding attendees sat back down in their chairs and waited for what was to come next. Lulu powered her beloved Eddie on and he beeped twice.

"I do," said Lulu, tears in her eyes.

Eddie beeped again. "I do, too," said Rosie, pulling a tissue out of the left breast pocket of her dress to wipe her bride's tears.

Eddie beeped in response and then they knew it. They were married. The ducks in the chairs all clapped.

Out of nowhere, there was a commotion on the street. Every duck rushed from sandy beach to the sidewalk, where they heard a sound they had never heard before. It was humans shouting, but they weren't angry.

"One! Two!"

"One, two, three!"

A marching band. A whole complete marching band with cymbals and tubas and everything. Here for the wedding? Must be.

The drum majors called the band to a halt and they all marked time in place. Some of the brass instruments were playing, but the woodwinds were clapping and dancing. Lulu and Rosie watched in awe as many of the players took their instruments from their faces and started to sing. They even broke away from their regimented form and danced over to where the ducks, and now curious humans, were standing. It was a marching band flash mob.

"Hey! Hey, baby!" they sang. "I want to know if you'll be my girl!"

After a period of singing and dancing, the members of the band marched back into their block formation and continued playing the song. Lulu could hardly believe it. She was a brilliant singer, but to march *and* play an instrument? It seemed impossible!

There was a quick feature of the low end, as the band members not playing all froze into a pose, then snapped back to attention. Lulu recognized the next part of the piece as eighth notes played by the wind players, and then once again the whole band yelled "HEY BABY!" And just like that, the fun was over. The band finished playing and the humans in the crowd cheered like they were witnessing the birth of Christ. There was a tap given by the drum line, which oddly resembled the woodpecker pecking on the window, and the band marched off.

***

Lulu and Rosie celebrated the day with champagne back in their hotel room. A few other ducks that they knew from back home joined them. The champagne was bubbly and it made Lulu loopy. She sloppily kissed her now wife on the cheek and promptly fell over. Rosie picked her back up.

"So what do we do with our wedding dresses now that the wedding is over?" asked Lulu, slurring her words.

"I suppose we could sew them into a blanket," said Rosie sarcastically. Lulu didn't catch the sarcasm in her boozy delusional fog.

The ducks all drank and laughed and reminisced about their summers back home: what they did, and what they saw. Rosie told the story of how she had accidentally stole a virtual pet toy for Lulu and how Lulu had then broken into their neighbour's house looking for a battery for it. In return, Lulu told the story of her big concert, and how only a squirrel had shown up. It wasn't funny then, but it was kind of funny now. Some of the other ducks told stories, too. They told stories of getting harassed by little kids and aggressive geese, eating dragonfly larvae, and getting fed by humans in paddle boats. Lulu and Rosie didn't want to relate, but they did.

Some of the other ducks tested out vaping for the first time that night, too. Instantly, they were hooked and wanted their own vape pens. Rosie sadly explained that she couldn't find tadpole-flavoured juice, but went on to talk about how the mint tasted just like a candy cane. Most of the ducks had never had a candy cane. Unless it was thrown to them by a human, they didn't deal much with human food. However, the vaping was an instant hit. It was probably the nicotine, but it pleased Lulu and Rosie to see the ducks acting more human than they usually did back home. For once, they felt understood by their peers.

The rest of the night was happy and celebratory. Lulu probably had a bit too much champagne to remember it clearly, but Rosie was living in the moment the whole time. They were in love, and that's all that mattered.

After a night of celebrating, the other ducks went back to all the different places they were staying for the winter, and the newly wedded pair were left alone in their hotel room. They went to bed in the morning, after staying up all night. Lulu's drunken stupor was fading away into clear thinking and consciousness.

"I say when we wake up we check out that rooftop pool," Rosie suggested.

Lulu, already asleep, snored loudly in agreement.

The sun was warm. It was a tropical paradise resulting in a very summery winter once again. And it was absolutely ideal they were embarking on this new journey together.

Fin.

About the Author

Gillian Corsiatto is a lifelong hobbyist writer, frequently recognized for her creative writing abilities, beginning at a young age. Her first job involved books and the written word, as she worked as a library assistant and page in her local library. In order to expand her writing skills and knowledge of literature, Gillian has taken post-secondary English classes, learning from accomplished professors. Outside of writing, music has been an important and constant aspect of her life, including taking piano lessons in early childhood, playing in college-level ensembles, travelling the world with a marching band, and playing solos for an online theatre production company.

Duck Light began with a friend of the author, who had a hobby of creating animals with human behaviours and characteristics. Her drawings would include imaginings like dogs standing on two legs and wearing clothing. At the time, Gillian found these creatures really weird, but almost in a near endearing way. Being no artist, but wanting to be supportive while trying something new, Gillian created a character of her own and called her Lulu. Because drawing is not the author's forte, she took Lulu the duck and turned her into words on a page. Gillian soon discovered it was actually kind of fun to play around with animal characters in this way. Duck Light is the result.

Gillian lives in Red Deer, Alberta with her beloved feline roommate, Aurora.